created by

Stephen Hillenburg

randomhousekids.com
ISBN 978-0-553-52088-0
MANUFACTURED IN MALAYSIA
10 9 8 7 6 5 4 3 2

nickelodeon™

CHRISTMAS TALES

A Random House PICTUREBACK® Book

Random House 🏠 New York

Contents

Happy Holidays, Bubble Guppies!

Adapted by Mary Tillworth
Based on the teleplay "Happy Holidays, Mr. Grumpfish!" by Adam Peltzman
Cover illustrated by Sue DiCicco and Steve Talkowski
Interior illustrated by MJ Illustrations

Hi! It's me, Molly. Tonight we're going to have a holiday party. It will be *fin*-tastic! Gil and I are going to deliver the invitations.

Here's an invitation for Mr. Grumpfish. Let's put it in the mailbox!

Next, we have to bake gingerbread cookies for the party.
Deema is the best baker ever! Yum! What's that delicious smell?

We're off to Marshmallow Mountain to get marshmallow frosting! We need lots of frosting for our gingerbread cookies. But we have to watch out for the Abominable Snowman! Do you see him?

The Abominable Snowman let us take the marshmallow frosting home! Now we are decorating a gingerbread house.

We hope Mr. Grumpfish comes to our holiday party.
He loves gingerbread!

It's almost time for the party. Look! Mr. Grumpfish is here!

At the holiday party, we give each other gifts.

We love opening presents, but we really love being together!

Happy holidays!

A Very Krusty Christmas

SPONGEBOB SQUAREPANTS

By David Lewman • Illustrated by Robert Dress

It was just before Christmas, and SpongeBob was decorating his house.

"There!" he said proudly. "Now let's pull the switch!"

"SpongeBob!" yelled Squidward when the lights came on. "How am I supposed to sleep with your lights shining like that?"

"Hi, Squidward!" called SpongeBob. "You're right. My lights need a little something extra. A blanket of fresh snow would be perfect!"

SpongeBob closed his eyes. "I wish for snow on Christmas Day."
He opened his eyes. "What's your Christmas wish, Squidward?"
   "To have the day off," Squidward grumbled.
   SpongeBob shook his head. "But the Krusty Krab is always closed
on Christmas Day."
   "Whoopee," said Squidward. "My wish has been granted."

The next morning, SpongeBob was all ready to decorate the Krusty Krab. "Mr. Krabs, when should I put up the tinsel?" he asked.

Mr. Krabs frowned. "Hmm . . . let's see. How about half past . . . *never*? Decorations cost too much."

"But, Mr. Krabs," sputtered SpongeBob. "It's Christmas! We *have* to decorate the Krusty Krab!"

Mr. Krabs folded his arms. "Give me one good reason, SpongeBob."

Just then, someone called out, "Look, everybody! The Chum Bucket has tons of Christmas decorations! And there's a huge line!"

SpongeBob and Mr. Krabs rushed over to the Chum Bucket.

"I heard there's a winter wonderland inside!" a customer said.

"Look at all the lights!" Patrick called out.

Mr. Krabs strode up to Plankton. "Your food's still lousy, Plankton. After the first bite, these customers will run back to the Krusty Krab faster than a flying reindeer!"

But Plankton just laughed. "Ha! Don't you know that at Christmas it's not about the food? It's all about bright lights and fancy trimmings! If you don't decorate, you won't make any money at all!"

Mr. Krabs gulped. "No money?" he said in a small voice.

Mr. Krabs turned to SpongeBob. "Well, what are you waiting for?"
he yelled. "Get back to the Krusty Krab and start decorating!"
SpongeBob grabbed Patrick's arm. "C'mon, Patrick, I need your help!"
Plankton watched them go. "This is going to be a very merry Christmas,"
he said to himself.

SpongeBob and Patrick got to work. "The Krusty Krab will be the most festive place in all of Bikini Bottom!" SpongeBob said.

"SpongeBob!" grumbled Squidward. "You're putting up way too many decorations! And what are you doing to that Krabby Patty?"

"Sprinkling it with edible, glow-in-the-dark glitter!" said SpongeBob.

Later, Patrick helped with the Reindeer Ride.

"Ugh!" he grunted. "It's hard being a reindeer, SpongeBob. I wonder how reindeer do this?"

SpongeBob smiled. "Don't worry, Patrick. It'll be easier once it snows."

"Is it going to snow?" asked Patrick.

"Of course," answered SpongeBob confidently. "That's my Christmas wish. What are you wishing for?"

"A hat made out of chocolate would be nice," said Patrick.

SpongeBob went back inside, where
Mr. Krabs was pacing back and forth.
"Aren't you done yet, SpongeBob?" he asked.

"Oh, no, Mr. Krabs!" replied SpongeBob. "We still have
to build the Christmas Fantasy Land, the Chestnut-Roasting
Center, and the Make-Your-Own Gingerkelp House Corner."

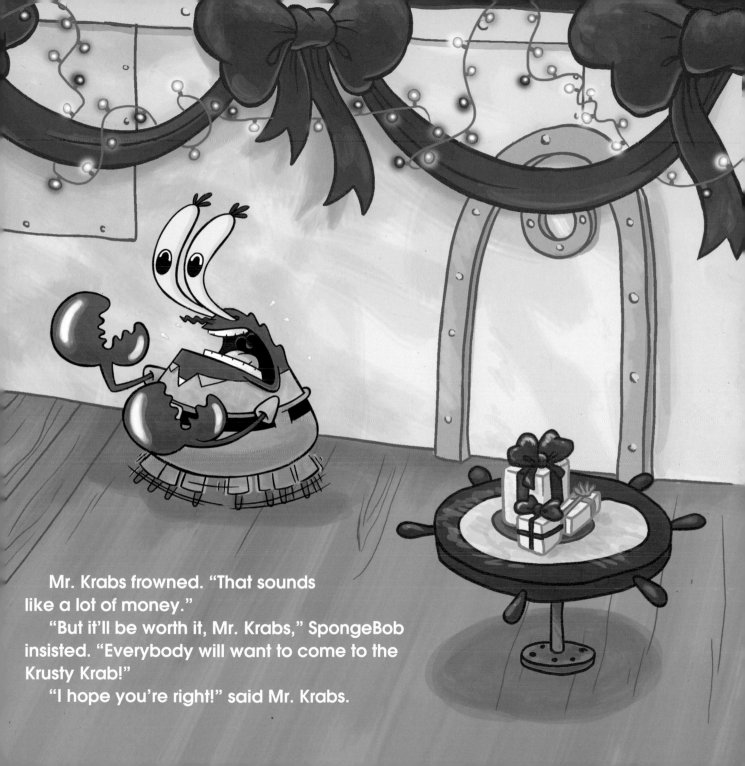

Mr. Krabs frowned. "That sounds like a lot of money."

"But it'll be worth it, Mr. Krabs," SpongeBob insisted. "Everybody will want to come to the Krusty Krab!"

"I hope you're right!" said Mr. Krabs.

The next day, it seemed like everyone in Bikini Bottom was at the Krusty Krab! They loved the Christmas decorations and activities—and they bought lots of Krabby Patties.

"SpongeBob, that decorating idea of mine was pure genius! Look at all the customers!" exclaimed Mr. Krabs.

"I know, Mr. Krabs," said SpongeBob. "Everyone's so happy!"

"Well, I'm not!" whined Squidward. "I can't wait till Christmas so I can enjoy my day off!"

Mr. Krabs shook his head. "What day off?" he asked. "With this many customers, we're staying *open* on Christmas Day!"

On Christmas Eve, SpongeBob and Patrick were outside the Krusty Krab, adding even more decorations.

Suddenly, Plankton appeared. "Happy holidays, boys! It's too bad Krabs won't let you decorate his restaurant."

SpongeBob was confused. "But, Plankton, we *did* decorate. See?"

Plankton looked at the Krusty Krab. "You call that decorating? I see a bare spot there and there, and there. . . ."

SpongeBob looked where Plankton was pointing. He was right! There was room for more decorations! SpongeBob quickly added several more strings of lights. Then he flipped the power switch . . .

. . . and the Krusty Krab went dark!

"SpongeBob!" Mr. Krabs yelled.

SpongeBob and Patrick ran into the Krusty Krab. But before SpongeBob could explain, he saw something very strange: a glowing Christmas bow scooting across the floor!

"It's one of my decorated Krabby Patties! It's alive!" SpongeBob said.

Mr. Krabs grabbed a flashlight and shined it on the runaway Krabby Patty—
and saw Plankton clinging to the bun! "Why, Plankton, were you trying to
steal my secret Krabby Patty recipe *again*?"

"And I would have, if it weren't for SpongeBob's stupid glow-in-the-dark
decorations!" Plankton said with a moan.

Just then, the sound of jingling bells filled the air.

Everyone rushed outside. It was Santa!

"Ho, ho, ho!" he chuckled. "Looks like someone needs a little Christmas magic!"

Santa reached into a small red bag and pulled out some genuine North Pole snow. He blew it at the Krusty Krab, and all the Christmas lights came back on. And then it started to snow!

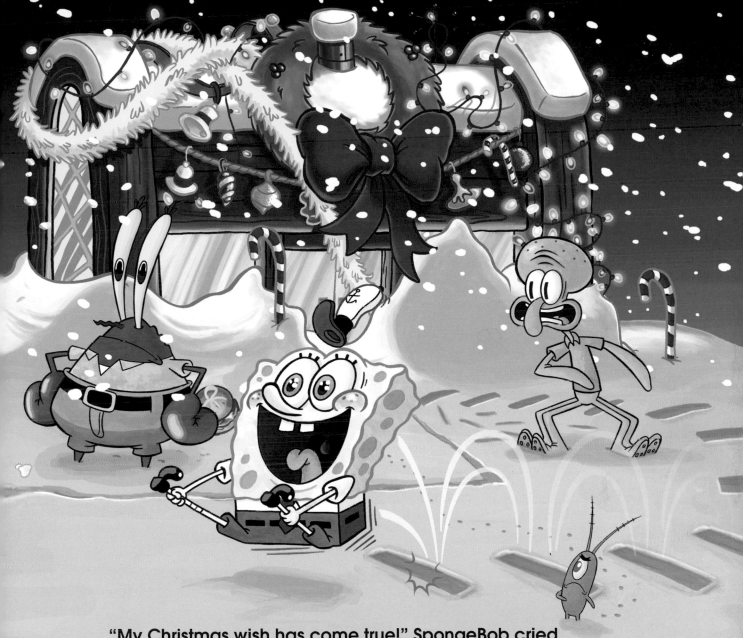

"My Christmas wish has come true!" SpongeBob cried.
Santa handed Patrick a present, which he tore open. "Oh, boy!"
shouted Patrick. "A hat made out of chocolate! Thanks, Santa!"

That night, it snowed so much that the Krusty Krab was closed on Christmas Day. SpongeBob shoveled his way to Squidward's house. "Merry Christmas, Squidward!" he said. "Your wish came true!"

"You're right, SpongeBob," replied Squidward. "Maybe there's something to this Christmas magic after all."

Dora's Christmas Star

Adapted by Mary Tillworth • Illustrated by Victoria Miller

t was Christmas Eve, and Dora and her friends were excited for their special Nochebuena party.

"It's my favorite night of the year!" said Dora. "I love to wear my holiday dress, decorate the tree, and celebrate with all my friends."

Everyone had worn their very best for the party. Dora twirled in her pretty red dress.

Boots adjusted his fancy purple bow tie. Isa's necklace sparkled.

"Let's decorate the tree!" said Dora.
Boots hung shiny Christmas ornaments. Isa strung twinkling lights. Tico draped tinsel. The tree looked beautiful!
Finally, Dora placed a shiny star at the very top of the tree.
"Our Christmas tree looks *perfecto*!" she exclaimed.

"Now let's put the presents under the tree," said Dora. She, Boots, and their friends worked together to carefully place the Christmas presents under the tree. The colorful wrapping paper glittered as the presents piled up.

Just then, Swiper appeared. He saw the pretty star on top of the tree, climbed up, and swiped it! "You'll never find it now!" he said, laughing as he threw it high into the air.

Suddenly, someone swooped down from the sky. It was Santa! He wanted to surprise everyone by coming to Dora's Nochebuena party.

When Santa saw that the star was missing from the tree, he knew Swiper had swiped it.

"Swiper, I've told you before, and now I must insist. Swiping on Christmas puts you on my Naughty List," said Santa.

"Remember what Christmas is all about," Dora told Swiper.
Swiper thought for a moment. "Christmas is about sharing and giving—not swiping," he said. He quickly found the star ornament high up in a tree and gave it back to Dora.

"Ho, ho, ho!" laughed Santa. "Swiper, you have learned the true meaning of Christmas. You are officially on my Nice List!"

It was time for the Nochebuena party! Benny brought tasty nuts for Tico. The Big Red Chicken brought Christmas cookies for Benny. Isa brought colorful flowers for everyone.

Dora and her friends ate *caramelos* and drank hot chocolate and danced and celebrated. "This is the best Nochebuena party ever!" said Dora.

Finally, it was time to go home. Everyone had had a great time at the party.

"I'm so glad I got to celebrate Christmas Eve with all my friends," said Dora.

"Merry Christmas! *¡Feliz Navidad!*"

Santa's Little Helpers

Illustrated by Bob Ostrom

Based on the teleplay "Santa's Little Fixers" by P. Kevin Strader and Jennifer Twomey

Do you see
a star?

It was Christmas Eve. The stockings were hung, and the tree was decorated. Team Umizoomi was ready for Santa to visit.

"I can't wait to see what Santa brings," Milli said.

Suddenly, the Umi Alarm rang.

Someone needed help!

Bot had a message on his Belly, Belly, Bellyscreen. It was from Santa Claus!

"Help, Team Umizoomi!" Santa said. "My toy machine stopped working, and we still need to make three more toys!"

"If the machine isn't fixed," Bot said, "Santa won't be able to deliver all the toys tonight!"

"We need to get to the North Pole and help Santa," Geo said.

"The best way to get to the North Pole is on a reindeer," said Geo. "I can make one with my Super Shapes! We need five triangles, one trapezoid, and antlers. *SUPER SHAPES!*"

"Glittering Gizmos!" Bot shouted as Team Umizoomi flew through the air on their reindeer. It got colder and colder. Snow started to fall.

At last, they landed at the North Pole.
"Look!" said Milli. "There's Santa's workshop!"

How many candy canes do you see?

Santa welcomed Team Umizoomi into his workshop. "Thank goodness you're here," he said. "The toy machine is broken, and we still have to make a sailboat, a dollhouse, and a fire truck."

"Don't worry, Santa," Geo said. "We'll fix this machine with our Mighty Math Powers!" Then he and the rest of the team climbed into the machine.

"To fix the machine," Bot said, "we have to know how it works. Let's check my Super Robot Computer."

The computer told Team Umizoomi that the first section of the machine was filled with buckets carrying toy parts. The next section was the Magic Duster, where the parts were put together. The last section wrapped the toys.

"Let's fix this machine!" said Geo.

Team Umizoomi found the part of the machine with the buckets. The conveyor belts were stuck, and the gears weren't turning.

Geo looked at the buckets. "First, we have to find the buckets with the parts for a sailboat, a dollhouse, and a fire truck."

How many green buckets do you see?

Team Umizoomi looked and looked—and they found the parts! Bot emptied them into a tube that was striped like a candy cane, and the machine started to work again.

"Now let's find the Magic Duster," Milli said.

The team quickly found the Magic Duster, but none of Santa's magic dust was coming out.

"We have to fix the Duster," Bot said, "or the last three toys won't get made."

"Look!" Milli shouted. "Those instruments play a special song that makes the dust come out. But one of the instruments is missing! I can fix this with Pattern Power!

"The instruments are supposed to make the pattern jingle bell, trumpet, trumpet. Let's see which one is missing." Milli studied the machine. "A jingle bell!"

Milli replaced the missing bell, and the machine started puffing magic dust that put the toys together!

The sailboat, the dollhouse, and the fire truck were finished, and they rolled into the Wrapper. Robot hands wrapped them in brightly colored paper.

"Hooray, Team Umizoomi!" Santa's elves cheered.
"You did it! You made the last three presents."
"Let's get these presents to Santa," said Geo.

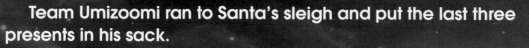

Team Umizoomi ran to Santa's sleigh and put the last three presents in his sack.

"Thank you!" Santa said. Then, as his sleigh flew into the starry night, he called out, "Merry Christmas!"

"I feel a celebration coming on!" Bot announced. Team Umizoomi and the elves danced in the snow and cheered.

SpongeBob SquarePants

Plankton's Christmas Surprise!

By John Cabell • Illustrated by Heather Martinez

One snowy day, Patrick went to SpongeBob's house.
"What are you doing?" he asked.
"I'm getting ready for Christmas," replied SpongeBob.
"That's great!" Patrick exclaimed. "Can I help?"

"Sure, buddy," SpongeBob said. "This is the most wonderful time of the year! And best of all, there's a big Christmas Eve party at the Krusty Krab tonight!"

When SpongeBob finished decorating, he and Patrick decided
to spread Christmas cheer and invite everyone they knew to the
party. They went to Squidward's house and knocked on his door.

"You're invited to the Krusty Krab for a party tonight," SpongeBob told him.

"You don't have to invite me," Squidward said. "I work with you. I have to be there."

SpongeBob sighed. "Work *and* a party? I love the holidays!"

SpongeBob and Patrick made their way to the Krusty Krab to help set up for the party.

"You know what the Krusty Krab needs?" SpongeBob asked. "A snowman—no winter wonderland is complete without one."

As Patrick rolled and packed the snow, SpongeBob
paused to catch a snowflake on his tongue.
    That was when SpongeBob heard something. . . .
It was a tiny, muffled voice.

Plankton popped out of one of the giant snowballs.
"Did I hear something about a Christmas party at the
Krusty Krab?" he asked. "Do you think I could come?"

of course you can come—the
merrier!" replied SpongeBob.
oody!" Plankton said, rubbing
ands together. "I wouldn't miss
world."

"Well,
more the
"Oh, g
his little h
for the

The party was about to start
Mr. Krabs was very excited.
"With so many payin' custo
and, um, good friends, how c
anything ruin the night?"

mers,
uld

Patrick hung the last of the garland as SpongeBob decorated a batch of gingerkelp cookies. Everything was perfect! Soon the guests started to arrive.

The party was a festive success! Everyone sang carols. Mr. Krabs gave SpongeBob a new spatula. SpongeBob gave Sandy a lasso. Then the doors swung open. Cold wind blew in.

A giant box tied with ropes stood in the doorway.
It seemed to roll into the restaurant by itself.
Suddenly, a little figure jumped up onto the box.

"Ho, ho, ho!" Plankton exclaimed. "When I was looking through my telescope last night, I noticed your tree was missing something, so I wanted to give you a surprise you'd never forget!"

Plankton opened the box. Inside was a single golden star with a cord and a plug.

"This is no ordinary star," he said as he carried the ornament to the top of the tree and plugged it in. It was the brightest star anyone had ever seen.

"It's the laser-powered Superstar 6000," Plankton announced. "I built it myself!"

"What's the catch?" Mr. Krabs asked, thinking Plankton was up to no good, as usual.

"Why, nothing, Krabs. Do you really think I'd do something evil on Christmas?" Plankton replied. But then he muttered to himself, "I'm saving *that* for New Year's Eve."